THE ADVENTURES OF MR POLKINGTON

The Adventures of Mr Polkington

by

Tina Rath

Mr Polkington descended from the omnibus and walked away from the lights of the main street, towards the big dark bulk of Rivenham Mansions, where he lived alone in a small dark flat. He climbed rather wearily to the fourth floor, let himself in, took off his wet coat, changed into his house-shoes, and went to the tiny kitchen where the daily woman had left his hot supper keeping warm between two plates on a low gas in the oven.

It would probably have been quite a nice chop, he reflected, if he had only managed to get to it an hour earlier. Mrs Wiggins really did her best for him. The flat might be small and dark but it was immaculately clean, and the suppers were always as good as could reasonably be expected. He carried the plate carefully into the miniscule dining room, and ate the withered chop and such of its accompanying vegetables as were not irrevocably sealed to the plate by a dried crust of gravy. He ate without particular relish, but he finished the meal, then carried his plate back to the kitchen, put it to soak in the sink and made himself a pot of tea.

Mr Polkington could easily have been what many of his business colleagues thought he was – the kind of middle-aged bachelor who has acquired, over the years, much of the fussiness of his female equivalent. Only a few of the older salesmen at the firm of Perkin and Warbeck's knew that Mr Polkington had once been married, and even fewer of those knew how that marriage had ended.

Mr Polkington had once been perfectly happy. He loved his young wife, Ethel, with the most perfect devotion, and she loved him. They had a little house in a quiet part of London, with a ridiculously small garden in which Mr Polkington tried, without notable success, to grow roses, and Ethel, with rather better luck, cultivated nasturtiums, and occasionally a fine crop of black fly. Sometimes they would have an evening at the theatre or a day by the sea, to eat sandwiches on the beach (except on those delirious occasions when they went to a café for fish and chips); more often they would visit Mr Polkington's sister, or Ethel's mother. And they thought they were perfectly happy. It was only when Ethel told him that she was expecting a baby that Mr Polkington realised it was possible to be happier, and when the baby was born, strong and healthy, and looking, to Mr Polkington's infatuated eyes, just like his beautiful mother, he knew that life had nothing better to offer. Ethel was inclined to suggest that such events as Baby's going up to Oxford, or becoming Prime Minister, or marrying a future queen of England, expectations which she saw as nothing less than his due, might be even better, but Mr Polkington doubted it.

Mr Polkington and Ethel were progressive parents. They believed in fresh milk, and fresh air, good food, and healthy exercise, and Baby thrived under this regime. Soon he was a baby no longer but a sturdy toddler, who grew more delightful and interesting every day. And they renewed their visits to the sea-side, where the little boy showed such a fearless enjoyment of cold sea-water that Mr Polkington determined he should learn to swim. So Ethel took him to their local swimming-baths, and they enjoyed their outings very much, until one day when the child seemed a little out of sorts when they came home. Ethel thought a night's sleep would set everything to rights, but by the morning he was very much worse, and Ethel, though she would not admit it, was by no means well herself. The terrified Mr Polkington called the doctor at once, who diagnosed a nasty, feverish cold, probably picked up at the swimming baths. But both patients grew worse and worse, and in an unbelievably short time, Ethel, who had refused to rest, collapsed.

She never really recovered consciousness, so Mr Polkington was spared one agony at least. He did not have to tell her when their son died. And a few hours later she died too. The doctor, who was old-fashioned and had no faith in the modern fads for exercise and cold water, probably did not mean to imply that Ethel and Freddy would still have been alive if they had not gone to the swimming-baths, but he managed to leave Mr Polkington feeling like a murderer.

Later, when he could think clearly again, Mr Polkington realised that he could very easily have ended up as a tramp, like those poor fellows he and Ethel had seen along the embankment on the nights of their theatre outings; those men who had always roused her sympathy rather than fear or disgust. He simply did not care what became of him, and on the day of the funeral he might have just locked his front door and wandered away.

But even at the worst, he did not quite forget that Ethel had loved him. He must be worth something. And for Ethel's sake he took care of himself. He sold the little house, although his sister would have moved in to take care of him if he could have endured the thought of another woman taking Ethel's place, and he got a good price for it, possibly because he cared so little about it. He sold or gave away all the possessions that Ethel and he had bought so hopefully together, and he rented his gloomy mansion flat in a part of London that he had never visited with his wife, and settled down to get through the rest of his life as best he could.

So now he sat, sipping his tea and reading the evening paper. He felt no particular interest in either world or local events, but he had always read the paper in the evenings, and he continued to do so. But, suddenly, and quite unexpectedly, he came across a name that did interest him: Perkin and Warbeck's, the name of his employers. Mr Polkington frowned. Respectable firms, like respectable people, did not, in his opinion, get their names into the papers. He began to read the news item with a good deal more attention than he had given an account of unrest in the Balkans. The Balkans never seemed to be very restful at the best of times, but this was the first time that Perkin and Warbeck's had achieved publicity.

And as he read, he discovered a very puzzling, not to say disturbing, story.

Apparently a young man, an employee of Perkin and Warbeck's, had disappeared. The last his family had seen of him was, Mr Polkington learned, the previous Wednesday morning, when he set out for his place of employment. His name was Percy Chiddock, and Mr Polkington had no difficulty in placing him. He was a plump, rather lazy young man, with an indefinable aura of grubbiness who, in Mr Polkington's opinion, would have been all the better for a few applications of cold water and Sunlight soap and a daily work-out with the dumb-bells. Mr Polkington was very much a senior salesman at Perkin and Warbeck's, and he had some responsibility for the training of the younger men. Mr Chiddock had *not* been one of his more promising pupils. It was, perhaps, a measure of his usefulness that Mr Polkington had not been aware of his absence for the past few days. The firm specialised in the supply of haberdashery and "notions" to the trade, and Mr Chiddock was not an ideal person to deal with young lady assistants in haberdashery departments. He was inclined to make equivocal remarks about the methods of storage of haberdashery materials, such as *"Have you got any of our fancy ribbons in your drawers, Miss Paxton?"*. He was disposed to leer. But he was not, in Mr Polkington's opinion, at all the kind of young man who was likely to disappear. Too much, he thought, of a mother's boy.

Even more disturbing was the reason why the police were taking his disappearance so seriously. He was not the first. There had been quite an epidemic of disappearing young men in the area. Now Mr Polkington was not a worldly man, in some ways, but he was no fool. He knew that young men might have very good reasons for taking themselves off, many of them not unconnected with young women (though again, surely not Percy Chiddock), but that would not account for so many of them, and all more or less at once. The police, he read, were pursuing the theory that the lads were being abducted by foreign seamen, to work as crewmen on Eastern voyages, but that hardly seemed likely to him. He had heard of professional sailors being decoyed aboard ships in need of crew, but he could not think that young men who had never stepped on board a boat, except possibly a Thames pleasure steamer, would be of any use at all for such purposes, however hard-pressed the captain. And if any foreign seaman, however devious and ruthless, could get an hour's useful labour out of Mr Chiddock, for example, he, Mr Polkington, took off his hat to him. But he did not for one moment believe that anyone would think of trying.

And there was another thing, a matter which actually affected him. He had not seen Percy Chiddock on the fatal Wednesday, but he certainly knew where he would have been going. Chiddock would have taken his appointments book with him, but the schedules of all the young salesmen were kept filed safely in Mr Polkington's memory. Perhaps the police would be interested in tracing his route, to pin-point, if possible, the moment when he deviated from it and vanished. He supposed, unwillingly, that he had better contact them as soon as he could. Respectable people did not have dealings with the police, any more than they appeared in the newspapers, but Mr Polkington knew his civic duty. He made a mental note to call in at the local police station as soon as he had a free moment next day, and then he folded his paper neatly and left it for Mrs Wiggins, who meticulously cut out any items relating to the Royal Family for her scrapbook, and used the remainder to polish her clients' windows ("*Nothing brings the glass up like newsprint,*" she had once confided to him) and went to bed.

In the morning Mr Polkington got up early and took his customary cold shower. He often told his younger colleagues that the application of cold water to the scalp stimulated the brain, and this morning he proved the truth of this axiom. He had thought better of his previous decision to go to the police with his knowledge of the last known movements of the missing Mr

Chiddock. No, he must not lay Perkin and Warbeck's customers open to the inconvenience of police questioning. It would be far better for him to make discreet enquiries himself and present the constabulary with Mr Chiddock's itinerary, complete with the point at which he ceased to follow it.

Mr Polkington arrived at the office in good time. In such good time, indeed, that he found himself alone there, and while he was waiting for his colleagues to appear he made a swift inspection of Mr Chiddock's desk.

There was nothing in the top drawer except some pieces of stationery, which Mr Chiddock had no right to have (upon which he appeared to have been keeping a record of bets – he clearly did not have an eye for a good horse), an apple core progressing rapidly towards mummification, and some half-eaten biscuits. Mr Polkington hoped it was the renegade Chiddock's teeth which had been nibbling upon them, but he was by no means sure. Really, if members of staff would leave food in their desks, it was hardly surprising if they attracted mice! Possibly a full desk inspection was in order. He emptied the first drawer into a waste-paper basket, and turned his attention to the others. These yielded nothing apart from a magazine of the kind sold in small stationers who also sold packets of unwholesome sweets and cheap fountain pens. He was about to send it after the rest of the detritus when it occurred to him that Mr Chiddock might have scribbled something on the inside cover, perhaps an address? He took it into his office for a closer examination. It was, after all, the only clue he had.

He spread the thing on his desk, and eyed it with considerable disapproval.

The title *FANTASTIC WORLDS* sprawled over the cover in blood red letters, superimposed upon a split picture: a dark haired lady whose unfashionably lavish figure was confined within a red dress so tight that she could not realistically have breathed in it at all was occupied in introducing a bright blue snake into a keyhole, while on the other side of the door a tall man dressed in jodhpurs was lying back in a leather armchair, peacefully enjoying a cigar. Surprisingly, the draughtsmanship was not at all bad. The figures, especially that of the lady, were nicely drawn. The hands were good. Mr

Pilkington, who had tried his hand at sketching when he was younger, had always had trouble with those. The snake was something of a disappointment, dangling from those realistic fingers like a length of ribbon, but on the whole the picture was well executed, although execrably reproduced. He raised the cover and, finding no clues at all in Mr Chiddock's hand or anyone else's, riffled through the pages. The reading matter was set in two columns in small and greyish type, which suggested, if nothing else, that there was not much wrong with Percy Chiddock's eyesight. It was interspersed with black and white drawings, evidently by various artists, whose work was by no means contemptible. The last few pages were given over to advertisements offering hair restorer, liver pills and similar items such as Mr Polkington prided himself that he had never felt the need for, as well as more dubious commodities, including correspondence courses in Hypnotism, Ventriloquism, or, more generally, the Mysteries of the Orient, all of which could apparently be learned in six weeks or your money would be returned. These he studied carefully. There was a possibility that Mr

Chiddock had been lured into danger by the offer of occult knowledge, remote though it was, but none of the would-be teachers offered addresses. You sent your request for enlightenment along with a postal order for five shillings – *five shillings! a week's wages for many people*, thought Mr Polkington – to a *poste restante* and if you were lucky received a few badly reproduced pages of nonsense, and definitely no refund.

He returned to the list of contents at the front and decided that the picture probably related to what must be the main story – a further adventure, apparently, in the life of one Captain Craddock – and read on. Again he was surprised to find both the spelling and grammar unexceptionable, and the worst errors, for instance the snake becoming a 'smake' and even a 'swake' at certain points, were certainly due to the printers. The story was nonsense, of course, but it was not wicked nonsense. The villainess introduced a poisonous snake through the keyhole of the library of Captain Craddock's club where he was enjoying a solitary cigar and locked the door. Our hero, however, escaped death by poison fang because he had, during what appeared to be his extensive travels in foreign parts, rescued the beautiful daughter of a snake charmer from the attentions of a libidinous rajah. Her grateful father had taught him a Word which tamed poisonous reptiles instantly, transforming them into loyal and helpful companions. Captain Craddock duly tamed the beast and put it in his pocket, before imitating the cries of a man fatally bitten by a Black Tailed Swamp Adder, a sound with which he was only too familiar, having lost more comrades in the Battle of Dalladalla to the native adders than to enemy action. (This would be *before* he met the snake-charmer, Mr Polkington surmised, otherwise he might have done something about it.) When the wicked but beautiful lady unlocked the door to gloat over his death agonies he leaped up, rushed past her, snatching the key in transit, and locked the door behind him before making his escape.

While Mr Polkington regretted this plot device, both as a bit of a *deus ex machina* and the waste of a good idea (he felt the author could have written the snake charmer incident up into another story, and possibly the Battle of Dalladalla too) he had to admit that the moral stance of the author could not be faulted. His hero had a properly protective attitude towards female virtue, and the snake charmer had shown the right kind of paternal gratitude. He felt Captain Craddock was unwise to put the snake into his pocket – who knew how the creature might react if it should fall asleep and wake to find itself in an unfamiliar environment? He himself would have suggested finding it a box (that cigar must have come from somewhere), but apart from that, he could not quarrel with the story. Captain Craddock had not used undue violence towards his would-be murderess, and she, he and the snake were all alive at the end of the story, presumably ready to appear in another episode.

Mr Polkington was a just man, and he admitted to himself that if a boy had the right stuff in him, this kind of reading would do no harm. He would soon leave it for the sunny uplands of Dickens and the healthy sea-scapes of Marriott, but no doubt it would set him on the path to reading. He doubted if Mr Chiddock *had* had the right stuff, but he could certainly have found more pernicious employments than reading this sort of material, nonsense though it was. Perhaps, of course, he had. Unfortunately the most careful examination of the endpapers and margins of the magazine revealed that he had not left even the most abstruse message behind as to what he *had* been doing. Mr Polkington would have to follow his original plan.

A quick examination of the papers he had left the day before assured him that he could easily take a morning to follow in Mr Chiddock's foot-steps. He took his own order-book with him and set out.

At first everything seemed perfectly normal. Percy had made three calls, and failed to pick up an order at any of the establishments he visited. Mr Polkington got two, and the promise that a third would "think about it, always providing they didn't send that young..." to them again. The fourth was quite a new establishment. New and splendid. Mr Polkington stood on the far side of the road, looking at the gilded Gothic lettering above the doorway, announcing the name (presumably) of the proprietor to be *Le Fanu*. There was an elaborate display in the double-window. Older and, he could not help feeling, more respectable establishments crowded their windows with goods, but they were tactfully obscured from the public view by warped glass and poor lighting. This window positively flaunted its contents. Something frilly, clearly feminine but of dubious shape, caught his eye, and he looked hastily away. And found himself looking directly into the eyes of a young lady who should, by rights, have been sitting at her own desk in Perkin and Warbeck's.

"Good Heavens!" Mr Polkington exclaimed. "It's Miss Throop, isn't it? Whatever is the matter, Miss Throop?"

For the young lady was standing in the street with tears running down her cheeks. She let out a small wail when she realised that he had recognised her. "Oh, Mr Polkington... I did go in this morning, but Miss Threadgold said I must go home because I had one of my heads."

"Yes, very well, Miss Throop, but why didn't you *go* home, then? Is something wrong? A relative taken ill perhaps? Can I be of assistance?"

"No one can help me!" Miss Throop wailed.

Mr Polkington glanced round. Miss Throop was becoming the subject of some attention from other pedestrians, and there was a respectable looking tea-shop on the corner. He gently cupped her elbow and steered her towards this haven. Before she could even take a breath to protest she found herself established at a corner table, well away from public view, and Mr Polkington was ordering a pot of tea for two, "nice and strong, if you please, as this young lady has had a shock. And a toasted tea-cake too, if you would be so kind. I feel sure," and he looked reproachfully at Miss Throop, "that she forgot to eat her breakfast today."

"There now," said the waitress. "Poor young thing. Would she like a glass of water?"

"Tea, I think, will be sufficient," said Mr Polkington. He smiled pleasantly at the waitress and she trotted off, shaking her head at Miss Throop's evident distress.

"Now, Miss Throop. Is this something you can tell me about, or would you," he coughed, "would you prefer to speak to Miss Threadgold? You know she would give you all the assistance in her power."

"Oh, it's nothing like that!" Miss Throop said, hastily. She knew what young ladies went to Miss Threadgold about. That lady was the Office Manager in charge of the lady typewriters, and her powers, though considerable, did not extend as far as Miss Throop's case at all. She blew her nose on a damp handkerchief and sat up straighter. "No. I'd like to talk to you, if you'll let me. And, please, don't Miss Throop me! It makes me feel so elderly and awful. I'm Violet."

And she thrust out her right hand. Mr Polkington blinked, then understood, and shook it. The child had a firm handshake, he decided. And, when she was not crying, she had a pretty face. Violet. Yes. Her eyes were indeed the colour of violets, though now they were violets filled with rain. The waitress arrived with their tea, and the warm tea-cake. Mr Polkington, firmly dispensing with any coy enquiries about who should be mother (in spite of her protests, he feared it might touch too painfully on Miss Throop's situation), filled two cups, adding milk and plenty of sugar.

"Drink that, my dear," he said. "You will feel much better if you do. And when you have finished it, you must tell me your trouble. If you can," he added hastily.

Violet obediently drank her tea and then, between healthy bites of her teacake, she began to speak.

"You see," she said, "I've been...oh, I don't know how to say it. Everything sounds so vulgar. Walking out...keeping company..."

Mr Polkington shifted uneasily in his chair, still wondering if this was actually going to turn out to be a case for Miss Threadgold after all. "Courting?" he suggested.

"Yes. Or whatever. Anyway, I have. With Cec— Mr Whiteside. You must know him. He's a colleague."

"A very good sort of young man," said Mr Polkington, only mildly stung by the use of "colleague" for someone so very much his junior.

"Oh, yes. He is. Or, at least, he *was*. Until he took up with that...that...Man Eater!"

"My dear young lady!"

"Well, she is. That's exactly what she is. She began with Percy Chiddock ..."

"Indeed!" Mr Polkington took a good pull at his own cup of tea and said, "Now, suppose you start at the beginning?"

And Violet told her story. Cecil Whiteside had been her young man. They had been walking out for only a year, but they had reached the stage of undergoing a formal introduction to each other's parents (a full complement in Violet's case, a widowed mother in Mr Whiteside's) and they might have announced their engagement by now if Mr Whiteside's mother had not been reduced to terrifying spasms by the mere suggestion of such a thing... and then suddenly, for no reason that Violet could imagine, her young man had dropped her. And taken to hanging about one of the young lady assistants at *Le Fanu's*, a nasty painted hussy who had previously entrapped Percy Chiddock and heaven knows who else if the truth were told, and now he passed Violet in the corridor of Perkin and Warbeck's as if he had never seen her before. And he had quite lost his appetite and looked so bad that his own mother had sent a note round to Violet, actually asking her to visit, to see if she could explain what was wrong, even hinting that she would consent to at least a discussion about a possible (long) engagement between Violet and Cecil, if that would bring him back to the man he had been. And now they were saying that Percy Chiddock had vanished from his home, and he'd probably made away with himself, and Mr Whiteside would do the same...

"But why should he do that?"

"Because of her of course," Violet said, "she takes men up, and, and…ruins them, then she casts them aside like…like worn out gloves, and they…well, I suppose they go and join the Foreign Legion. Or something worse."

Mr Polkington nodded, but he wondered if there could be a more sinister explanation. Perhaps the young woman was indeed extravagant and heartless, inducing her suitors to spend money on her that they could ill afford, so that they got themselves into enough debt to make any young man run away. And, of course, there were worse possibilities, possibilities which could not even be breathed in the presence of a young lady like Miss Throop… the dreadful word *infection* formed itself in Mr Polkington's brain. He had no idea how long such terrible diseases took to show their ghastly symptoms, but surely sufficient time hadn't passed for them to manifest themselves in Mr Chiddock, and certainly not in Mr Whiteside… unless Mr Chiddock had indeed discovered that he was ill, and *warned* Mr Whiteside…

He waved the waitress across and asked for the bill. "You sit here and finish your tea," he told Violet, "it appears to be a most respectable establishment, and I am sure you will not mind staying here alone for a few minutes. I am going to take a look at this young lady. In which department does she work?"

"Ribbons and Notions," said Violet, "will you...will you speak to her? I was going to. I really was. But...somehow I couldn't summon up the courage."

"I'm not sure," said Mr Polkington frankly. "I'm not at all sure what I should say. But something rather unpleasant seems to be going on, and I think I have a duty to investigate."

He paid the bill, giving the waitress sixpence and asking her, in an undertone, to keep an eye on Violet, and crossed the road to *Le Fanu's*. At least he had the perfect excuse for doing so, and he was not, as so many men might have been, intimidated by the feminine atmosphere.

Two ladies were standing, heads together, looking at an array of silk and satin ribbons that a young female assistant had tossed across the mahogany counter for their admiration. They were probably intended for a wedding-dress, for they were in all shades of white and cream, and even to a man of Mr Polkington's experience they all appeared more or less identical in quality, colour and width, but the three women were very intent on comparing and contrasting them and Mr Polkington was able to observe the young assistant at his leisure. At first glance he was inclined to agree with Violet's estimate. She was indeed a painted hussy, with elaborately puffed hair and wearing, he suspected, a Young Venus corset beneath her neat black shop assistant's gown, with its nun-like touches of white, an effect which quite defeated its original demure intention. It was easy to see that an impressionable young man might find her extremely attractive. And then, perhaps feeling his gaze upon her, she looked up, directly at Mr Polkington. Their eyes met. And he stepped back, feeling the sweat break out on his upper lip, knowing that he was looking at Death.

He was not sure how he got out of the shop, but moments later he was grateful to find himself sitting next to Violet in the tea-shop, being offered a glass of water by the sympathetic waitress.

"Oh, Mr Polkington, whatever has happened?" Violet was saying.

"I...don't know," he said, his voice sounding shockingly hoarse and strange to his own ears.

He took the water from the waitress gratefully, and drank. He was frightening the women, he told himself, and he must pull himself together. The glass was gently taken away from him and a cup of tea – hot, strong and with a whiff of brandy – was substituted. He would have waved it away, but the girl said, "Go on. We keep a bottle behind the counter, for the fainters," and he sipped gratefully.

"There's something funny going on over there," said the waitress. "Isn't there?"

"I think so," said Mr Polkington. He was grateful to hear that his voice sounded more like his own.

"What is it?" Miss Throop wailed. "Oh, what is it?"

He shook his head. Not for anything would he tell these two nice young women what he had sensed behind the pretty, painted mask of the shop-girl in *Le Fanu's*. He could hardly describe it for himself. He had been aware of a kind of horrible hunger, a grey void that would draw all laughter, all joy, all kindness, all life into itself and annihilate it if it could. And that horror was stooped over the pretty young bride and her mother...

And what could he do about it? Call a policeman and tell him what he had seen, what he had *felt*? They would lock him up. A clergyman? He might be kind, he might listen, but he would certainly end by suggesting that Mr Polkington should consult a doctor. And the doctor would call in a colleague, and *they* would lock him up. Perhaps, of course, they would be right to do so. Perhaps the girl was quite innocent, quite normal and he was mad. But in his heart he knew that he was not. And whatever stood at the ribbons and notions counter in *Le Fanu's* was not a girl at all. It was something that might have stepped out of the pages of one of Mr Stoker's more exciting works. But where, where, would he find a Professor Van Helsing to deal with it?

"I'm sure that Cecil is meeting her to-night," Violet Throop said in a small voice.

And Mr Polkington made a rather courageous decision.

"Do you know where?" he said.

"No," said Violet, and then, with equal courage, and even more determination, "We will have to follow him."

"*We* shall do no such thing," said Mr

Polkington. "I shall do so, but I will do it alone." Miss Throop opened her mouth to protest, but he continued, firmly. "Miss Throop, I am giving you what is perhaps the hardest task. You must go home and wait for news." He did not quite add that this had been the lot of women throughout the ages, but the suggestion did hover in the air between them. "Will you require my escort, or are you able to make the journey alone?"

Miss Throop caught her breath. "I shall go alone. Cecil is working at the office today. Please, please, hurry back and do not let him out of your sight."

"I promise you that I shall not. Now, shall I find you a cab?"

"No," said Miss Throop, falling suddenly back into her seat. "I would like to stay here for a few minutes to collect myself. Please, go to Cecil."

"You leave her with me," said the waitress. And Mr Polkington, faced with two determined women, did just that.

He returned to Perkin and Warbeck's as quickly as he could, and established that Cecil Whiteside was safely on the premises. It was fortunate that his office, a small room with a large glass partition, had been arranged to enable its occupant to keep a discreet but close supervision of the younger occupants of the larger outer office, and Mr Polkington sat down to perform various routine but necessary jobs and to keep an eye on Mr Whiteside. It is, perhaps, a tribute to Mr Polkington's orderly and disciplined mind that after he had the young man safely under his eye, the first thing he did was to log the orders he had taken that morning, and make a note of the establishment that should have another visit. But after that he found he could not concentrate sufficiently to find himself anything to occupy him usefully. Instead he took out Mr Chiddock's copy of *Fantastic Worlds* and flicked listlessly through it, looking up every so often to make sure that Mr Whiteside had not left his desk. It was probably not ideal reading for someone who only that morning, he believed, had come so close to the realities that these writers treated so lightly. All you needed was a grateful snake charmer and a powerful Word to disarm Horror. Wave a wand, or a stake, at it and it would dissolve. Or you could carry the power in your own person. Mr Polkington found himself reading about yet another chap, who, like Captain Craddock, had travelled in the more exotic parts of the world, and learned to harness the Power of the Light, a power which he tossed with cheerful abandon into the faces of human and supernatural villains, always with the same gratifying effect.

He wondered just how he was going to handle his encounter with the horror. What could he do? *Reason* with it? Clearly not. But perhaps he could reason with Cecil, persuade him to leave the creature of his own accord. And then what? Allow the creature to maraud about London...but of course, he was being a silly old fool. What he should do was go home, perhaps in time to eat his supper before it became hopelessly dessicated, and enjoy a cup of tea and the paper like a sensible man...

Mr Polkington only realised that he had struck his clenched fist against his desk and growled "Coward!" when startled heads looked up and round in the outer office to see what the disturbance was. Seeing nothing untoward the young men went back to their work, and Mr Polkington pulled himself together. No, he did not know what he was going to do, or even if there was anything he *could* do, and his spirit failed within him at the thought of going anywhere near that horror again, but he must try. For some reason he remembered something from his childhood, someone – an uncle, a friend perhaps – talking to his father one evening. He vaguely thought the man was an officer in the Fire Service and they were talking about a near disaster that the older man had averted. He was insisting that he had simply done what was necessary. Whatever it was it was not going to happen, he said. 'on *my* watch'. Percy Chiddock had, perhaps, been lost on his watch. But he would not lose another.

But it was growing late. He put *Fantastic Worlds* aside and prepared to spend the next hour or so keeping an eye on Cecil Whiteside. That young man had remained at his desk for the whole afternoon. He had not indulged in any of the office banter. His voice was not heard in the general discussion on the quality and sufficiency of biscuit supplied with afternoon tea by Perkin and Warbeck's. A casual observer might have supposed he was a quiet and hard-working young man. But Mr Polkington's experienced eye informed him that he had done no work at all.

Nevertheless he remained at his desk, still doing nothing, when the other young men began to leave, calling cheerful and occasionally ribald good nights to each other as they did so. The blue London dusk came down and turned the windows into mirrors, so Mr Polkington could see his own anxious face hovering ghost-like behind Mr Whiteside. But Mr Whiteside, staring at the scratched and splintered wood of his desk, saw nothing. Or perhaps, Mr Polkington thought, he saw too much. At last he stood up, threw on his hat and coat, and slouched out, with Mr Polkington following him at a close but careful distance.

He seemed to move through the brightly lit streets like a sleep-walker, avoiding collisions with vehicles or fellow pedestrians more by instinct than by any conscious intent. He was certainly not hurrying eagerly to meet his lady, but neither was he loitering. And he appeared to know exactly where he was going. Mr Polkington wished that *he* did. They had already moved out of the district that Mr Polkington knew well, full of large, respectable shops and comparatively neatly dressed people, and into an altogether more unpleasant neighbourhood.

The streets were darker and narrower, and such passers-by as he met seemed to slink rather than walk, and some eyed Mr Polkington in a rather disturbing way, as if they had an interest in the possible contents of his wallet or the potential value of his watch. Once a shockingly young girl actually laid her hand on his sleeve and asked if he were looking for some company, but his look of horrified pity was sufficient to make her back away. He began to wonder how he would ever find his way home.

And then, at the end of a narrow street, he saw what might have been a vista of bare trees but, he realised at once, were actually the clustered masts of shipping. They had come to the river. Mr Polkington saw his quarry hesitate and then move forward into the golden pool of light cast by a gas lamp that burned on a high blank wall. And out of the shadows came the creature he had last seen on the ribbon counter of *Le Fanu's*, and moving to wreathe her arms around the young man's neck.

Mr Polkington had hoped that he might be inspired to do what was necessary to rescue Cecil Whiteside when the moment came. He felt no such inspiration, but nevertheless he stepped forward and exclaimed, feebly enough as it seemed to him:

"Leave that young man alone!"

She drew back a little and showed her teeth in a kind of snarling laugh. "Go away you dried up, useless old man! What have you to do here?"

"I was given charge of this young man's welfare, and of the other whom I fear you have already made your victim. I have failed once but I will not fail again."

And he stepped forward into the light. The boy was standing quite still. His face was very white and looked curiously empty. Mr Polkington wondered if he was already too late.

"Who gave you the power to see me as I am?" the creature demanded, staring at him. "You are no adept."

"No, indeed," said Mr Polkington firmly. Whatever an adept was, it did not sound the right thing for a respectable man to be. "I do not know. Perhaps because I once learned to know goodness in a woman I can also recognise evil. I can see you for the foul and unnatural thing that you are, and I shall stand between you and this poor young man for as long as I can stand at all."

"Not so very long then," the creature said, and

reached for his throat. For a moment Mr Pilkington was overwhelmed by the most dreadful draining sensation of horror and fear. He wanted above all things to stand back and avoid the touch of that creature's fingers.

But instead his feet took him forward, and out of the shadows in the street behind him erupted two figures, two young women in fashionable hats who closed in on the creature, screaming, "Leave him alone, get away, get away!"

And he realised that both Miss Throop and the waitress had followed him just as he had followed Mr Whiteside. At all costs he must protect *them*. He felt a sudden burst of energy, and lifting his hands he called on the Light, like man in the story, knowing it for cheap fiction, knowing it was useless... Even when it happened he thought it was an illusion, a last effort of his brain to blot out the horror before him, but the pain was no illusion. Rays of light and energy were indeed streaming from his raised hands, but they burned more terribly than any earthly fire he had ever encountered. The pain was intolerable, and the fear that his hands would be charred away, leaving him hopelessly maimed –

if he survived the pain – almost worse, but the conviction that the Light was real kept him upright, kept him directing the fire towards the creature. And it felt the flames. A terrible keening wail broke from its lipless mouth, and it burned, melting away until there was nothing left but a heap of sodden, evil smelling rags upon the cobbles. Miss Throop gathered them up with the tip of her umbrella and tossed them over the embankment into the river.

Mr Polkington stood, whimpering helplessly, gazing at his hands; unburned, unblistered and still hurting like...even in his thoughts, Mr Polkington was aware of the presence of ladies and told himself they 'hurt like billy-oh!'

He was not at all sure what happened after that, until he found himself in the back room of a dockside tavern, drinking a cup of hot, black stewed tea that seemed to him as strong as the brandy he had tasted that morning. At some time along the way the pain in his hands had ebbed, but now he felt as weak as a kitten and needed both hands to hold his teacup. Mr Whiteside, already coming out of his strange trance, was sitting on a window seat being quietly reconciled with Miss Throop and the waitress was talking softly with a woman in a vulgar lace trimmed blouse and tight black satin skirt who must, he thought, be the landlady of the place. She was rouged and powdered in a way that would normally have shocked him, but now he could look beneath the surface and see that her face had the beauty and dignity of a nun. When he looked up she came and laid her hand gravely on his shoulder.

"I couldn't do nothing," she said, softly. "I knew there was something like that about but I'm getting old and tired, and I knew it wasn't no use me trying. We needed someone like you."

"I... it was the young ladies..."

"They helped. And I did my bit, but we needed you. And we'll need you again."

"So the Light was real, then? But how could a piece of cheap fiction..."

"You stood up to defy evil, that was real enough and all that mattered."

Mr Polkington wanted to ask more, but the sound of wheels outside interrupted him, and Miss Throop bustled them all out to a cab which had somehow been obtained for them in an area where, he felt sure, few cabs were usually to be found. He realised afterwards that he did not even know the name of the tavern, nor would he be able to find it again. And he was almost glad of that.

He went back to his dark little flat, ate his supper, and went to bed, where he slept dreamlessly, although when he woke the next morning he was almost ready to believe that everything had been a dream. But there was that residual soreness in his hands which did not wear off for several days. And the announcement of the engagement of Miss Throop and Mr Whiteside, who seemed already to have forgotten, only sometimes smiling at Mr Polkington when they passed him in the corridors as if he had been a favourite uncle. Although they could not have explained why.

Most extraordinary of all was the reappearance of Percy Chiddock, discovered the next morning outside the premises of *Le Fanu*, with no recollection of where he had been or what he had been doing for the past week. Except that he knew he had not enjoyed himself, and somehow the experience had convinced him that the life of a salesman was not for him. And for some reason he knew he owed a debt of gratitude to Mr Polkington. His mother despatched him to the country to 'help out' an uncle who had recently bought a chicken farm.

Mr Polkington, conscientiously exercising his stiff fingers, knew he had had a glimpse of the real powers and dangers that lay below the everyday surface of life and, remembering the woman's words, he wondered, a little fearfully, when he would be needed again.

Mr Polkington sat at his desk in his office at Perkin and Warbeck's (Haberdashery and Notions), wondering how he was going to spend his Saturday afternoon. He could hear the young people hurrying out of the building, and thought he could detect more hilarity than was usual, even for the beginning of the weekend holiday. Perhaps it was the influence of the Spring which had come so suddenly to the London streets on this March day. Old Mr Warbeck, who had wandered into his office for a gossip (and was one of the reasons why Mr Polkington himself was not hurrying out into the pale sunshine) walked to the window and said, "Daft lasses!"

Mr Polkington hastened to look for himself, disturbed by this suggestion. But all he could see was a group of young lady typewriters, perhaps a little more flowery in the hat department than was quite usual, making their way down the street

"They're taking young Violet Throop to a cake-shop to get her drunk on tea and buns," Mr Warbeck said. "She's leaving us. Getting married. To one of your salesman. Quite a family celebration for us."

Mr Polkington nodded. He knew about Violet Throop and her young man. Perhaps rather more than Mr Warbeck did.

"Eh, I remember when I was a lad in Milltown, when one of the weavers was getting wed they'd pin ribbons all over her dress, put a wreath of paper flowers on her head, and a veil if they could get it, and parade her like a maypole from pub to pub. But it's the same thing, though, underneath."

Mr Polkington nodded again, but more doubtfully. He could not imagine Miss Threadgold, the Office Manager in charge of the young ladies, allowing such a thing.

"That Violet's a pretty girl, and she'll make a pretty bride. And so she should. Every item of her wedding clothes at cost price, as you might expect. Even the shoes, though that's a bit surprising in haberdashery. But Miss Threadgold's got her contacts, apparently. I went into their office this morning and there's the whole crew of silly girls gazing at a little pair of white satin slippers as if they were holy relics ... I don't know what they'd have done if she'd brought the veil in – we'd have had no work from them for the rest of the day, I daresay."

As it happened Mr Polkington knew that Miss Throop *had* shown her wedding veil to her female colleagues earlier in the week. And even Miss Threadgold had been seduced from her desk to offer her pinch of incense at the shrine of bride-worship. He had walked into her office and seen her spreading the delicate stuff between her fingers, marvelling – lace as fine as spider silk, she had declared, worked all over with cream-coloured roses, while the young ladies whispered about the wedding dress, repeating mystic words like "oyster satin" and "demi train" to each other, and he had crept away, fearing to profane their mysteries.

"They came up to our office, saying they were getting subscriptions for a wedding present for the pair of them and Mr Perkin said he couldn't understand why any young woman with a steady job, earning fifteen shillings a week in a respectable establishment, would want to give it all up to get married. 'It's a good thing they do,' I told him, 'or where would your next lot of lady typewriters and salesmen come from?' To say nothing of the fact that a quarter of P & W's own business is in the wedding line. And then he wrote himself down for three guineas, which meant the rest of us had to do the same or look like pick-farthings. They should have enough to buy them a house."

"That would be no bad thing," said Mr Polkington seriously. "It isn't always good to start your married life living with your parents."

"Not when you'll be living with Widow Whiteside, that's for sure. She cornered me behind one of the floral decorations at the last staff jollification and told me about her spasms," he shuddered. "I tell you, the last time I felt like that was when my nephew was down from Oxford for the Christmas Vacation," he tempered this shockingly boastful statement with a wink at Mr Polkington. "He *would* take me and his young brothers to the *Theatre des Horreurs*, brought over from France for the season. Better than a panto, he said it was. And there were a pair of old hags in that, shrieking about and killing folks with knitting needles, that might have been Old Mother Whiteside's born sisters. Tell young Cecil to take her to audition for them the next time they come over."

"Good Heavens," said Mr Polkington. "Did the lads enjoy it?"

"Fair lapped it up. O'course they bit the liked best was when some big lass stripped right down to the kind of undergarment we *don't* have in our catalogue. French I suppose. Young Robert said it was a body-stocking, and I did wonder how he'd know…still, he assured me it wasn't mucky. It was so they could do something clever with lights that made her look as she was going green and decaying before your eyes."

Mr Polkington made a private resolution to avoid this kind of theatrical entertainment at all costs.

"You'll have young Robert under your charge, come autumn. He finishes his degree and he's going into the business, starting from the bottom, just like me and Mr Perkin did in our time. And glad to do it, the young devil! 'I shall have rooms in Piccadilly, and my own money in my pocket,' he says, 'and won't there be larks!'"

"Rooms in Piccadilly..."

"I told him he'd likely have *one* room in a boarding house in Bloomsbury, and like it, and 'Well, Nunkie,' he says, 'Bloomsbury's quite *close* to Piccadilly...'"

He turned back to the window as a faint sound of singing drifted up. The young ladies, safely away from the strict but fair supervision of Miss Threadgold had begun to sing '*Here comes the bride.*' "Daft lasses!" He blew his nose with unnecessary vigour. "Well, I'll be off now. Enjoy your afternoon, Polkington. All work and no play – you know!"

He wandered off. Mr Polkington sighed. He knew he must be a very dull boy indeed, for play hardly featured at all in his life. It was hardly to be expected that it should. He had a moment's sadness, hoping that Violet Throop and her young husband would enjoy their happiness for longer than he and his Ethel had done, then he shook himself. There was no sense in allowing himself to become morbid. It was a lovely spring day, and he must use it for something better than allowing himself to fall into a fit of the dismals. Instead of going home to his tiny mansion flat where the sunshine never penetrated, he would go for a walk. And because, for him, a walk *must* have an objective, he would make for that tea-shop where he had first spoken to Violet Throop. It would be a pleasant stroll, taking him through the emptying streets of the City, and across the park. Once there he would allow himself to drink a small, sentimental toast in tea to Violet's happiness before he went home alone.

He put on his coat and hat and went down into the warm afternoon. Several times during his walk he wondered if he had made the right choice. The City streets were bright, but already empty, with the curiously unused and, it must be admitted, *unwelcoming* look they had at weekends. The park, in contrast, seemed very full of couples strolling happily together. Some, and it was those who struck Mr Polkington to the heart, had young children with them... but he walked on steadily, telling himself that if he was to become distressed every time he saw a happy family he had better set himself up as a hermit or a lighthouse keeper at once. But he was grateful when he came to the tea-shop and he could sit down quietly in a corner.

Perhaps the tea-shop owner had felt a breath of spring too. There were pretty embroidered cloths in evidence, and his table was decorated with a tiny bunch of violets in a jar. Mr Polkington waited for someone to take his order, and he was a little surprised when, instead of a question, he was presented with a pot of tea and a toasted tea-cake. He looked up to see the waitress who had played quite a part in the rescue of Violet Throop's fiancé from the 'creature' who had very nearly lured him to his destruction. Somehow he had forgotten that she might still be there.

"I hope it's to your satisfaction, sir," she said, indicating the tea-cake.

"Ah. Yes. Thank you very much. I...well...I ..." he found he was stuttering under her grave regard. Then he said, "I haven't come here by accident, have I? I thought it was a whim of mine, but I suspect I have been *led...*" *and I know I am talking nonsense,* he added mentally, wondering what could be happening to him.

"Yes, sir," she said, quietly. "You are needed again. But it's your own choice, sir."

He thought of the almost intolerable pain he had suffered in his last encounter with the supernatural – and found himself saying, "But of course, I choose to help. If I can."

Her face, neither plain nor pretty, but so ordinary that you might pass her a hundred times in the street without recognising her on the hundred and first, was illuminated suddenly by her smile. "I knew you would. Do drink your tea, sir, while I get my hat..."

"No," said Mr Polkington firmly. "Please fetch another cup, and sit down so that we can drink our tea together." He made a sudden decision, and added, "My name is Alfred."

She brought the cup and sat down, hesitantly. "Mine is Mollie... er..."

"Alfred," Mr Polkington interrupted firmly. He cut the tea-cake in half and offered her a piece. "Now Mollie, you must tell me what this is all about."

She crumbled the tea-cake unhappily in her fingers. "That's just what I can't do, s— Alfred. Sukey says..."

"Sukey?"

"She's the landlady of the *Ship Ashore*. You remember..."

"Ah. Yes."

"She says there are people who have looked

further into the dark side than others. And if they look fearlessly into the dark they can learn to call on the light."

"People who have looked into the dark," he repeated. He felt a sudden spasm of grief and rage. So he had lost his wife and son, and in exchange he had been given this foolish power. And then he looked at Mollie. There were tears in her eyes.

"And you have looked into the darkness too," he said, gently.

She nodded.

"And you would rather not talk about it. Instead you must tell me what I am needed for. Is it another...?" he hesitated, still not sure what to call that Grey Death he had banished into the river.

"That was something of the sort of thing they used to call a werewolf, Sukey thought. But no, it's not that. It's best if she tells you herself," Mollie said. She stood up, shaking the crumbs off her skirt. "If you're ready, sir."

He was clearly not going to get any information about what he was wanted for. He did not ask again, but waited while Mollie put on her hat, threw a cover over the counter, drew down the shop blinds, locked the front door, and led him out through the back way, locking that door behind them too. Looking round he realised that they were in a small, cobbled alleyway that seemed somehow to have very little to do with modern London, with its electric lights, its motor-buses and its tea-shops.

"We might almost have stepped back in time," he said.

"Sometimes I think we can," Mollie said surprisingly. "There's layers and layers of London all round us. And times when you come on a place where the top ones have been peeled away."

She set off, leading Mr Polkington through streets that he was quite certain he had never seen before. They were cobbled underfoot and dark above, with buildings whose upper storeys sometimes almost met across the street, shutting out the sky. And their footsteps seemed to make no sound as they walked. But there *were* sounds; singing, talking, street cries and the rumbling of carts, all at the very limits of hearing, as if they were incomprehensibly far away.

Much, much sooner that anyone might have

reasonably expected, Mr Polkington saw that grove of trees growing from the river, the masts of shipping, and he realised that they were making for *The Ship Ashore*.

He had never seen the little dockside tavern by daylight. It looked surprisingly neat and respectable for its surroundings, and it had a large, elaborately painted sign, depicting a sailing-ship in a country lane, fitted out with a door and a smoking chimney, surrounded by other strange images: a cat chasing a dog up a tree, a man nursing a baby, and at the door of the ship a sailor could be seen turning away in horror from the triple temptation represented by a buxom young woman holding out a foaming tankard and a pack of cards. Mr Polkington smiled and followed Mollie inside.

The few drinkers hardly glanced up as he and Mollie crossed the room and went up the stairs behind the bar which led to the landlady's private rooms. Perhaps, he thought, they were used to strange visitors. Sukey stood up as they came in, and kissed Mollie affectionately.

"You got here very quickly," she said.

"We took a short-cut."

Sukey laughed. "Came by one of your back-doubles, did you? Well, sooner you than me." She turned to a girl who was sitting at a table by the window, writing, "Pearl, duckie, can you fetch us some tea and then go and watch the bar for a bit?"

When Pearl stood up Mr Polkington was taken aback to see how beautiful she was. She had a mass of very lustrous, very straight black hair, tied back with a red ribbon, forming a rich background to a lovely, delicate face, a wonderful complexion and slightly tip-tilted eyes. It was a beauty made all the more incongruous by her bottle-green school uniform.

"My grand-daughter," Sukey said as she left the room. Her shoulders stiffened, as if she anticipated disapproval. "Her grandpa – my husband – was a Chinese gentleman, as you can probably see from her looks."

"She is a very lovely young woman," Mr Polkington firmly.

Sukey's shoulders eased a little. "He was a very good looking man. And no woman could have had a better husband. He knew something about...these affairs too. I...learned from him. He went out to America to work on the railways there. He sent money home as faithful as faithful, which is how I came to buy this place. But they were using explosives – blowing up great rocks. And...he got hisself blown up. They never found him, nor any of the men working with him. I knew something really bad had happened to him when the money stopped, but I never knew what it was for a year or more, until a friend of his came back here to tell me. He told me it wasn't nothing to do with the dynamite but they'd somehow got the wrong side of a dragon. I didn't believe him then. I thought it was the shock had made him silly like. Only later... I knew."

They were all silent for a moment while Mr Polkington wrestled mentally with the idea of dragons interfering with the construction of the American railway. Or perhaps it was a *Chinese* dragon, who had come *with* the workers...

"And then Lily – my girl – Pearl's mother," her voice broke.

"Please don't upset yourself," Mr Polkington said gently.

"No need to say any more, Sukey," Mollie said. "He's looked into the dark too. He knows."

Mr Polkington looked round for a distraction

and found it in the exercise books Pearl had left behind. The pages were covered with what appeared to be complex mathematical formulae. Mollie caught his startled eye.

"Pearl's a very clever girl, Alfred," she said.

"She is that," said her grandmother. "She goes to ever such a good school in Camden Town, and if she's a good girl and works hard they say she'll get to one of those new ladies' colleges."

For a moment Mr Polkington thought of those commercial colleges where Perkin and Warbeck's lady typewriters learned their skills, but Mollie said, with an almost maternal pride, "Oxford, they think. Or Cambridge."

Pearl came in softly carrying a lacquered tray with a teapot and an assortment of small bowls. "And I shall be a Professor of Mathematics," she stated in an accent which mingled – not unattractively – the true notes of docklands with an overlay of gentility from her Camden school. *And so she will* thought Mr Polkington, and somewhat overcome, he sat down and allowed himself to be served with a bowl of hot, straw-coloured tea. It smelt oddly perfumed, and there was neither milk nor sugar in evidence, and he was not sure he would like it, but courtesy compelled him to try. It was unexpectedly pleasant. Pearl looked round to make sure everyone had been served, made a graceful movement something between a nod and a bow to her grandmother, and withdrew, silently, down the stairs.

"Now, ladies," Mr Polkington hinted.

"Yes," Sukey said.

"It's not easy," Mollie said simultaneously.

And both women fell awkwardly silent. Finally, and most unexpectedly, Sukey said, "It's not very nice I'm afraid."

And Mollie said, "It's the time of year."

Mr Polkington, quite out of his depth, shook his head.

"Today," Sukey said, "is the spring equinox. One of the two days in the year when the hours of darkness and the hours of light are exactly the same length."

"It's supposed to be a good time for ritual magic," said Mollie with a slight sniff. "Nasty goings on," she added.

Sukey took a long breath. "And Pearl told me about this girl in her class at school. Young Joan. A nice little thing she is, got no mother, and her father calls hisself an artist, but he's more like a drawing-master, if you ask me..."

Mollie sniffed again.

"Well, she told Pearl she was a bit unhappy about something. Her pa had been taken up by a real artist. Quite famous he is. Calls himself Cyprian De Morteville but I doubt that's the name his mother and father gave him..."

Mr Polkington, that indefatigable reader of his daily newspaper, had certainly seen that name and exclaimed, "But he is quite a shocking person! Wasn't his last exhibition closed down by the police?"

Sukey nodded, grimly. "He paints nasty pictures all right. And some of them – some of them tell those with an eye to see that he knows a bit more than his prayers. Oh, not as much as he thinks he does, I dare say, but... something. Well, he picked out an acquaintance with Joan's pa at an exhibition of some of his and his students' work. *He* would have it that this Cyprian recognised his talents, but *she*, and she's got more sense at her age than he'll have at ninety, thought it was more likely that he saw some sketches of *her* being as how she models for her pa and his students..."

Mr Polkington shook his head.

"Because he tried to make up to her. Brought her presents. Tried to talk to her alone. And finally says he wants her to model for *him.*"

Mr Polkington shook his head. "Surely her father..."

"She complained to him right off, and he wouldn't do nothing, says the chap's only being kind and she's got to be polite to him because he's got influence and could do all sorts of things for him. Either he's got no sense at all or, well, I don't want to think what else. Well, she doesn't want to model for him, only of course her pa says she's got to. The chap can get him introductions, get his pictures sold he says again, and she mustn't be selfish. So in the end she agrees and she goes along a couple of times with her pa's housekeeper, so-called, to chaperone... *She* used to model until she got past it, and she's not what I'd call a *nice* woman... anyway, the girl liked it less and less. She's got to wear this black dress and a black lace veil with a wreath of poppies, 'sposed to be the Bride of Death or some such, and lie on this altar affair... there's a gutter in it, she says, like it might be for blood, and a nasty kind of knife lying on it, beside her..."

"How very unpleasant!" Mr Polkington exclaimed.

"And he never lets her see the picture, well a lot of artists don't. But the last time he was called away and the house keeper – *so called* – was asleep in a chair, and she did take a look. She'd thought he might not be painting anything at all, just sort of, *staring at* her, which she didn't care for, as you might suppose, but when she saw the picture she liked it even less. It was of her all right. Of her with her throat cut. Very ugly she said it was, with a lot of blood. And something nasty *lapping* at it."

Mr Polkington gave an inarticulate exclamation of horror.

"She nipped back behind the screen they've got there, and she was getting out of her costume when he came back. She never let on what she saw. But then he asked her to come back for one last sitting. Today. Must be today, and late afternoon today, just before sunset, because of a certain sort of light he needs. And she's to come to the back door, which will be open, because there won't be anyone to let her in, and he may not hear the bell...oh, and he might not be in the studio, but she's to get ready, and take the pose, and wait…And the housekeeper can't go with her…got to see her old mother in hospital. Or so she says. But pa still says the girl has to go…"

"And of course, she must not!" Mr Polkington said.

"No, she won't. She's gone to her aunty in Hampstead. That's her pa's sister, but she hasn't spoken a word to him since she got married, him taking against her because her husband's in trade, and the husband taking against Joan's pa because he isn't, well he's not doing any kind of job that the uncle thinks a man *should* be doing, anyway, so she'll be happy to take Joan in, and she won't be in any hurry to send her back, they having no children and the aunty always wanting a daughter." She stopped for a moment then, with an effort she went on, "But if she doesn't turn up at all I'm afraid he'll have another girl lined up. Because I've got a feeling that it's not just murder he's got in mind. It's a sacrifice. He's going to cut some poor child's throat at sunset today. It's part of a magical pact. To give him power."

"I cannot believe in such things," Mr Polkington exclaimed.

"But there are Powers," Mollie said. "Bad ones as well as good. It's not *what* he's doing that will make Them give him what he thinks he wants. Bless you, you can't *make* Them do anything. But maybe it amuses Them, pleasures Them, whatever, to make him commit such wickedness. Then They'll have Their claws deep in him, and he'll dance to Their tune, all the time thinking he's a great magician, commanding the Powers of the Air. Or whatever."

"And so They'll have a puppet ready to commit any kind of nastiness. Which we must *stop*," Sukey said strongly. "We must save Pearl's friend, of course we must. But we must do it without him knowing that we're on to him, until it's too late for him to find another victim."

"Then you can face him down and order him to stop trying to work dark magic. Which he will. Got to, by the rules he thinks he has to follow," said Mollie to Mr Polkington.

Mr Polkington thought about "facing down" a murderer, a solid human being, possibly a younger man, and one with a penchant for knives.

"And," said Sukey, as if she knew something of what he was thinking, "They won't like it neither. You'll have taken two victims from Them, that poor young Joan, not that she's Theirs, and never will be, but They'll want her fear and pain, and the wasting of a young life that might have come to something, that's just the kind of thing to please Them, *and* you'll have stopped Their games with Their silly dupe. I'm not saying it's safe..."

"But I see that it has to be done," said Mr Polkington, surprising himself. "I hope that I am the man to do it."

He heard the women sigh, gently. Sukey stood up and went quietly to the door. "Pearl dear, can you come up here a minute?" she called.

Pearl came in, silently and stood in the middle of the room, her head bent, that strange, lovely face veiled by her long hair.

"Pearl's going to help too," said Mollie.

The girl lifted her head. "He wants a model," she said. "D'you think I'll do?"

"That is out of the question..." Mr Polkington began.

"Joan's dark, like me," Pearl said. "And I'll be covered up in that dress and veil. He'll never know the difference until it's too late. We'll give him the fright of his life."

"I hope so, duckie," Sukey said.

Did she sound dubious? Mr Polkington wondered. He felt uncertain enough himself...

"Well, we'd best be off," Mollie said. "The studio is in Chelsea so we're going by boat."

She led them down the stairs. Sukey followed them, and took up her place behind the bar in the almost deserted pub. Mr Polkington looked back to see her standing there, her ringed hands lying on the polished wood, and again, in that curious double vision he remembered from their last encounter, he saw her as austere, remote as a praying nun.

"Sukey is doing her bit for us," Mollie said, as if she guessed his thoughts. "And there are others..."

How many, he wondered, and where? Probably the driver of the steam launch waiting for them at the bottom of a flight of wet steps, who received them in silence and set off up the river as soon as they had sat down. It was late afternoon. Soon, he supposed, it would be sunset. And then...

The journey seemed very short. They stopped at another flight of steps, and Pearl ran up, followed more sedately by Mollie and, much less briskly, by Mr Polkington. He had a sudden dull conviction that this was all nonsense. They were making a fool of him – worse, he was making a fool of himself. He was about to say so when he realised that Mollie was looking at him anxiously.

"No!" she said sharply. "It's real! Believe it!"

The girl ran across the road. Mollie followed her, and Mr Polkington trailed behind, still trying to tell her that it was all nonsense and he was having no more to do with it. But there was a part of him that knew he had to keep walking, to follow the two of them. There was a door in a high fence in a side-street that opened when Pearl pushed it. It led into a garden, neglected and curiously frostbitten in spite of the spring sunshine, and at the end of the garden another wall and another door that let them into the house.

"Empty," said Mollie. "He's sent the servants out. Most of them..." she added, uneasily.

The first thing Mr Polkington noticed was the unpleasant smell. *The place hasn't been properly cleaned for years*, he thought, not given a good turn out to scrub the old memories of past dinners and ancient cats, and perhaps worse, out of its fabric. It was stale, grubby, and wholly disgusting. Pearl seemed to feel the nasty atmosphere, because she was moving more and more slowly, climbing the backstairs with dragging feet. And Mollie had stopped altogether. She actually sat down on the stair, breathless.

"There's something really horrible here," she gasped. "You go on, if you can. I must..." she leaned her head against the banisters. By now Mr Polkington could think of any number of reasons for them to leave the house at once, and Mollie's evident illness was probably the most pressing one. But Pearl went on, and he could not let her go alone.

Then they came into the burst of light that was the studio. It struck Mr Polkington that the heart of the unpleasantness he felt in the house was here, although it was bright enough, and clean too, if you excepted that ugly stained block of grey stone set up in the middle; the altar that Sukey had mentioned, he supposed. Pearl darted behind the screen, and Mr Polkington looked around for a hiding place. A rack of costumes set up against the wall seemed adequate, and he positioned himself behind it.

Moments later Pearl emerged, dressed in that thin black dress and veil – *an ugly parody of a bride* thought Mr Polkington, with a shudder. She adjusted her poppy wreath and lay down.

For a moment nothing happened. But in that moment Mr Polkington had plenty of time to think... to think that he *must* leave the house. He was probably the victim of some stupid plot, got up between Mollie and Sukey and Pearl, and the absent Joan, if she existed at all. Blackmail might be the least of it. And Mollie, on the stair below them, was almost certainly having some kind of stroke. He should take her to hospital, find her a doctor... The voice telling him these things was eminently reasonable. It was not his own voice, but that hardly seemed important. And then the glass roof of the studio flooded with red light as the sun began to set and they were standing in the heart of a blazing lantern.

A door opened at the far end of the studio, and the artist walked in. Mr Polkington's doubts dissolved. The man was wearing an elaborately decorated robe of red silk but it was open at the front to show a great deal too much of a plump, naked body... and he was carrying a curved dagger. Mr Polkington, shocked beyond words, stepped out to intercept him, but before he could tackle him Pearl rose up from the altar. She caught the man by his knife hand, pulled him smoothly forward and threw him, somehow, over her shoulder to sprawl across that horrid altar. The knife dropped from his suddenly nerveless grip and skidded across the floor.

At the same moment the red light died. And Mr Polkington realised that he had been brought in, not to protect Pearl, who could so manifestly protect herself, but to defend the would-be magician. Something huge and horrible was stooping above the studio, blocking the light from the dying sun, concentrating on him like a beam of black light.

"Run downstairs, Pearl, and look after Mollie," Mr Polkington said clearly. "No, don't worry about getting changed..."

The girl obeyed him. He was not sure if she was aware of the danger, but she was a good, sensible girl and she obeyed. The magician was scrabbling about the floor blindly, trying to find his dagger, whimpering out what might have been prayers. And still that horror beat on him. There was a disgusting *enjoyment* in it, Mr Polkington thought, as if something was rejoicing in the man's terror. And what it was going to do next, which would cause so much *more* terror. And real physical pain. A kind of drooling, idiotic, *dangerous* enjoyment... and when it had finished with the failed magician it would turn on him too. He remembered how once, when he had been out for Sunday stroll with Ethel, they had come across a group of boys surrounding a cat. They had exuded just that feeling. He had wanted to hurry Ethel away, but she had been braver than he. She had turned on them with such a righteous blaze of anger that they had withered under it. And she had rescued the cat...

Mr Polkington accepted that he could never be as brave as his wife had been. And that Cyprian De Morteville was probably a much less worthy object of rescue than that cat... but ... but... He clenched his fists (quite stupidly, of course, you couldn't *punch* an evil Power) and said aloud, "Leave him alone. You have no business here."

Cyprian stopped scrabbling and whimpering. To Mr Polkington's horror he crawled to his feet and crouched there as if it was a place of refuge.

"Go along now," said Mr Polkington. *I sound like a policeman*, he thought – *one of the particularly thick-headed sort, too.* "This man has rejected your bargain. He wants no more of your false promises." He longed for that white fire which had seemed to spring from his finger-tips to defeat the werewolf, even with the pain that it had brought him, but there was no sign of it. "And you have been roundly defeated by a couple of school-girls..." He unclenched his fists, and lifted his hands. *Might as well try*, he thought... And suddenly a different light blossomed between his hands. The crimson light of the sunset burned painlessly on his palms. It broke through the darkness and spread, enfolding him and the magician crouched at his feet – not the white stabbing, cleansing light of his last encounter, but warmth and protection, spilling from his cupped hands, "You have been beaten," he repeated with more confidence. "Go. Leave this place." The light burned through the darkness. "The children were always safe from you. And now the man has repented of his folly and he too is under the protection of a power immeasurably greater than yours, or mine, but which allows me to speak for it. You have failed."

The light filled the room, and it was the last of the sunset.

Cyprian De Morteville stood up. He looked down in horror at his robe, and in some embarrassment at Mr Polkington.

"I seem to have been making a bit of a fool of myself," he said.

There were explanations and, inevitably, strong hot tea made in that grubby kitchen by the now recovered Mollie (*after* she had rinsed out the kettle, and washed the cups and teapot). She had also found a small maid-servant, who had been asleep – much too *deeply* asleep – in the attic, as she informed Mr Polkington grimly. She did not need to labour the point that she would probably have been Joan's substitute. The girl was still very sleepy still, but accepted, with remarkable docility, that she was to drink some tea and then go home to her mother with the kind lady.

Mr De Morteville, clothed and more or less in his right mind, was hugely apologetic. He realised that he had offended against the proprieties, but it was quite plain that he was not at all sure how. He hardly seemed surprised to find himself sitting in his kitchen with a pretty school-girl, a waitress, one of his own maids and a salesman for haberdashery and notions. But he seemed to know, however vaguely, that he owed them a great deal. Especially Mr Polkington. He vaguely tried to offer them money.

"No," said Mr Polkington as firmly and kindly as he could, "the best way you can repay us is to take care not to get involved in such things again."

"No," Cyprian said, earnestly. "Of course... I shall... I shall take up gardening, I think. And a different sort of painting. Landscapes, perhaps. And I must pay more attention to my housekeeping. This place must be thoroughly cleaned. I cannot think how I allowed it to get into such a state."

"Quite right," Mollie said. "Emily here will come back tomorrow, with the rest of them, and make a start. Hot water and plenty of soda. That's what you need. And you can dig over the garden, just as you were saying. You will find yourself quite different afterwards. Work up a good sweat, and take cold showers. Nothing like a cold shower. Oh, and I'd get rid of that altar if I were you. Or give it a good scrub and break it up to make a rockery. A few hours work with a sledge-hammer will do you the world of good."

Cyprian nodded and then said, vaguely, "I suppose one can buy a sledge-hammer at Harrods. Or perhaps the Army and Navy Stores."

"I would certainly think so."

"I sent the servants away. I'm sure I don't know why. Perhaps I had better go to a hotel for the evening."

"You'd much better go with this gentleman," Mollie said.

And so he did. Mr Polkington, after seeing him safely bestowed in a bedroom at *The Ship Ashore* and putting Emily and Mollie in a cab to see each other home, sat down at last in front of a late supper with Sukey and Pearl. Noodles, accompanied by various strange, unusual, but by no means unpleasant flavours formed the basis of the meal, and Mr Polkington was surprised to discover how much he preferred it to Mrs Wiggins' suppers and wondered how she would feel if he were to provide her with some recipes ... but he was grateful to find he was given a knife and fork rather than the sticks which Pearl and Sukey employed so deftly.

They ate at length in a companionable

silence, until Mr Polkington felt he could ask a question that had been troubling him.

"How did you contrive to knock a grown man off his feet like that?" he asked Pearl. "Was that... *magic?*"

Pearl shook her head. "That was unarmed combat. I learned from my Auntie, Radiant Blossom. Our headmistress wants her to teach it at gym classes. She says all girls should learn. You never know when it might come in useful."

Mr Polkington, taken aback as none of the events of the day had so far taken him aback, could find nothing to say.

Mr Polkington was not comfortable. It could have been the weather. The warm early spring had turned into an unseasonably hot summer. The trees in the park, which had been such a fresh, hopeful green a few weeks ago, were already looking dusty and tired, and Mr Polkington was feeling rather dusty and tired himself. Perhaps, he thought, he needed a tonic. He certainly felt that he needed a change. His work at Perkin and Warbeck's, which he usually performed with conscientious cheerfulness, was becoming almost intolerably wearisome. But it would be a long time before he could even think about a holiday, and really, at his time of life, holidays were nothing much to look forward to.

Of course, the root of his malaise was boredom. He had, in the past few months, been introduced to a strange new world, frightening but exciting; a world where, it seemed, he exercised considerable powers. And now he was back in the every-day, trying to turn three particularly lumpen young men into a sales force to be reckoned with. Three young men who, he had quickly discovered, had nicknamed him "Aunt Pol."

He was unwilling to admit it, even to himself, but he had found himself visiting the tea-shop where everything had started, only to find it shut and melancholy, with dead flies lying on the window-sills, and its pretty tablecloths hanging grubby and neglected on the empty tables, whatever time of day he tried it. And he could not find *The Ship Ashore*, the dockside tavern which seemed to be the centre for the strangeness he had experienced. Mr Polkington, a salesman to his backbone, could trace any address in London, but he could not find that tavern. The name, he discovered, was not a common one, and of the few he had found none – including *The Ship Aground,* which he had included just in case – were the one he was looking for.

He began to seriously wonder if he had been

suffering from delusions. What more likely than a lonely man, of no particular importance, should invent exciting adventures for himself – based, he had to admit on a collection of stories in a sensational magazine – and then begin to believe them... adventures in which he was the heroic rescuer... Mr Polkington determined to pull himself together and find himself an interest.

His grief for his lost wife and son was still too raw to allow him to return to the kind of things they had enjoyed together, the outings, the swimming... but he and Ethel had rather prided themselves on being modern, so Mr Polkington decided to throw himself into the very opposite. He embarked upon a study of the history of Ancient Rome.

If he had not been feeling so uncomfortable, he would probably have acknowledged this as a mistake very early in his studies. The Ancient Romans seemed to have divided their time between wars (which he considered a dreadful waste of time, and a wicked waste of lives) and a kind of domestic misbehaviour which he found both shocking and incomprehensible. Why, he wondered, when Caligula announced his intention of... well, whatever unsuitable and unmanly piece of behaviour he *did* intend at the time, did a couple of those large, grave, elderly men with beards who appeared so frequently in Roman sculpture not intervene to prevent it? One to each elbow in the time-honoured method of dealing with those not in proper control of their senses could easily have conducted him to a darkened room, where he could have "got over it." But the Romans had too many hot baths, he suspected, and not enough cold showers. And there was insufficient attention paid to women, whose influence could be so important, and so healthy... he imagined that Miss Threadgold, for instance, would have dealt with the likes of Caligula in *very* short order.

But having embarked on his studies Mr Polkington soldiered on. He even spent a Saturday afternoon in the British Museum, conscientiously gazing at large white pieces of carved stone, and trying to spark an interest in their originators. But at the end of several hours all he had acquired was sore feet, a nagging head-ache, and a deep desire for a cup of tea which, as he wandered through the tangle of streets surrounding the British Museum, seemed unlikely to be satisfied until he had travelled the considerable distance between himself and his mansion flat. There *were* teashops, but this being a Saturday afternoon they were, unsurprisingly, all closed, and clearly intending to remain so until Monday morning. Mr Polkington was about to give up and search for a bus stop when he turned into a small street he had not seen before and saw a lighted shop window.

It was probably a book-shop, he told himself wearily, and indeed as he drew closer he saw there *were* books in the window, along with some curious star-patterned drapery that looked as if it belonged in a conjuror's act, a dusty crystal ball and some candles. But there was a gap in the starry drapery, and through this he could see at least one table and some chairs, and overcoming a strange feeling of reluctance (this was, after all, exactly what he had been looking for) he tried the door. It opened and he found himself inside a small shop. The first thing he noticed was the *smell*, an unpleasant mixture of mildewed books and a smoky perfume, which could only be incense. He was turning back to the door, telling himself that this was certainly not the right place for him, when a woman swathed in shawls and tinkling with a good deal of silver and amber jewellery rose up from behind the table.

"You are a seeker," she informed him in deep and thrilling tones.

Mr Polkington would have liked to reply, rather crossly, that he was merely seeking a cup of tea, and he had clearly come to the wrong place, but courtesy – especially courtesy to women, however eccentric their appearance – was too much a part of his nature. He did, however, in his rather confused apology and attempted withdrawal, mention *tea*.

Her face lit up instantly. "The tea leaves! Of course. I don't get asked for those very often, but they have a long tradition – a long tradition – please, sit down and I shall be with you in a jiff."

Mr Polkington sat down and the lady rustled out, trailing shawls and scarves. He thought, briefly, of flight, but that would have been rude. And besides he had no idea of the length of a jiff. It would have been extremely embarrassing to have been caught half-way out the door. But as he was casting a yearning glance at the doorway, it was suddenly filled and darkened by the figure of a man. For a moment it looked really quite sinister... and then he stepped into the light and was revealed as a very young man, almost a boy, dressed in a style that Mr Polkington's professional eye identified instantly as cheap but flashy. Literally flashy, for his large tie-pin, in the shape of a scarab beetle, set with a large red stone with pretentions to be a ruby that deceived no one, caught the light with an ominous, bloody glint.

"Anyone taking care of you?" he asked, staring at Mr Polkington. Somehow he made it sound like an insult.

"Yes, thank you," Mr Polkington said coldly, wondering why he had taken such an instant dislike to the man.

The woman rustled back into the room with a tray. The hands which gripped the tray trembled a little.

She heard him come in, Mr Polkington thought, *and she is afraid...*

"I was just making some tea," she said quickly, "the gentleman requested the tea leaves."

"Oh come off it! Tea-leaves! Not that old biddy stuff. You're not working on the pier at Brighton now, you know."

The woman winced and bit her lip. There was surely no need, Mr Polkington thought, for that nasty jeering tone. "I most certainly did ask for some tea," he said firmly.

"Drink it then," the lout said, "and come upstairs. You're a parlour client you are and it shouldn't take a psychic to see that."

Mr Polkington wondered, nervously, what kind of establishment he had strayed into. 'A parlour client' sounded quite improper. Almost indecent. But the woman was holding a tea-cup towards him with an imploring look and he knew if he left now this unpleasant young person would somehow 'take it out' on her. He accepted the cup and drank down the contents, lukewarm and stewed though they were, replacing the cup on the tray with a smile with which he tried to convey thanks and reassurance. Then he followed the young man further into the room and up a dark and narrow stair, keeping a firm grip on his umbrella in case it was needed as a weapon of defence.

He was half-expecting to be introduced into some kind of satin boudoir, and prepared to make it quite clear that there had been a mistake, but much to his relief he found himself in what looked like a gentleman's study, dominated by a large leather-topped desk. The walls were lined with bookshelves, except where tall, uncurtained windows looked out over a green square. Mr Polkington sniffed – the whole thing struck him as bogus. He would not have been surprised if the books had been purchased by the yard. But the young man was looking round complacently, as if sure that the room was making the right impression. He threw himself into the leather armchair behind the desk and sprawled inelegantly, nodding for Mr Polkington to sit down too. He did so, reluctantly. The man was impressing him more and more unfavourably by the minute. He had a very poor complexion, combined with languishing dark and slightly protuberant eyes. *And* a poor physique, suggesting late nights and a shocking lack of exercise.

"Who sent you to us?" the man asked.

"No one sent me," Mr Polkington said stiffly. "I saw your window and assumed – foolishly no doubt – that I might get a cup of tea here."

"Thought we were a teashop!" The man gave a raucous laugh. "That's a good one."

Mr Polkington had a shocking notion that

this unpleasant person might lean forward and nudge him in the ribs. Instead he busied himself with choosing a cigar from a box in front of him, snipping the end with a pair of silver cutters, and striking a match from an ornate silver box. Only when it was well alight did it occur to him to push the box across to his visitor.

"No thank you," Mr Polkington said. "I do not indulge."

"Saves you money I suppose," the man agreed. "You wouldn't credit the price of these…"

Mr Polkington, sniffing the unsavoury fumes, thought he could hazard a guess at both price and actual value.

"Welllll," drawled his host, "let's pretend you don't know me. Just walked in thinking we were a tea-shop, eh!"

He seemed to find this so genuinely amusing that Mr Polkington wondered if he had inadvertently used some kind of *code*, but he finished his laugh and leaned forward, saying, "Here's my card."

The card was, of course, elaborately but rather badly printed. It announced – in three different fonts, Mr Polkington noted – that the owner was "George James Fortescue-Homes,

Medium and Psychic." He was only surprised it did not add "to the Nobility and Gentry."

A hand (with a large ring, set in this case with a green stone gripped in the mouth of a serpent whose tail formed the body of the ring) was thrust across the desk, and Mr Polkington found himself shaking it. "How do you do," he said. "My name is Polkington."

"Doing well, thanks for asking," said Fortescue-Homes. "Well, I don't have to ask *why* you came to us. You've got an aura like a lighthouse."

Mr Polkington winced.

"Fair *pouring* out the energy you are," he went on. "Want a tip? Sit like *this*" he twisted himself into an ungainly position, hands clasped, one foot crossed over the other. "Seals the exit points, if you get my meaning. Stops the energy leaching away. Now..." he disentangled himself and began to scrabble energetically in one of the lower drawers of his desk, "I know what you've come to see, and I won't keep you waiting. Yes," he said, apparently misinterpreting Mr Polkington's puzzled expression, "I just keep it lying in a desk drawer. Not in a safe. Safes are asking for it. Burglars go straight for them."

He regained a vertical position, holding something covered with a green silk cloth carefully between his hands. Mr Polkington, intrigued in spite of himself, waited for him to unveil the secret. He would not have been surprised by anything, he thought: a human skull, the Holy Grail, a fortune teller's crystal or, more probably, some indecent picture – and then, he *was* surprised. Because what Mr Fortescue-Homes produced was a small glass jar, a baby version of those great green and purple jars that old fashioned chemists still kept in their windows, but it was a glass jar shot full of flashing, coloured lights. They rippled over the walls and ceiling, the colours changing, brightening and fading as Mr Polkington looked. It was a most extraordinary effect, and Mr Polkington wondered mildly how it was done.

The young man set the jar down reverently on his blotter. The lights whirled even faster and shot rays of purple and crimson. Mr Polkington felt, obscurely, that it was *angry*. But that was ridiculous. It wasn't alive... it couldn't be.

"There," the young man said, "the Fortescue-Homes Receptor."

"It is certainly...remarkable," Mr Polkington allowed.

"Touch it," the young man offered. "Go ahead. It's not an offer I'd make to just anyone, but seeing as how it's you..."

Almost against his will Mr Polkington stretched out his hands and cupped them round the flashing belly of the jar. He was aware of feeling something – nothing so positive as a tingle or a warmth, but *something*, something almost like the very beginning of those occasions when he had drawn Light into his hands to combat evil. The lights swarmed towards his fingers, beating against the glass like imprisoned fire-flies. He snatched his hands away, and immediately felt he had made a fool of himself by doing so.

"Ahhh," breathed Mr Fortescue-Homes, "you feel it, don't you? And *it* feels *you*..." He tossed the green silk veil over the jar, but the lights shone through the silk.

"What does it do?" Mr Polkington breathed.

"What doesn't it do? I haven't found its limits yet," said the young man. "But...watch." He scrabbled in the drawer again and produced a matchbox. He opened it and shook out a small, rather crumpled looking spider. He turned the jar so that a crimson ray fell on the creature, which curled up its legs, jerked once or twice, and died. "And that's not all," the young man whispered. "Cup your hands round it and *ask* for what you want... *ask*... money, women... you'd be surprised at the women I've had..."

Mr Polkington heard a thundering in his ears, and realised that it must be his own heartbeat.

"So," Mr Fortescue-Homes was saying, "do you reckon we can do business?"

"Business..." Mr Polkington floundered. Was he being asked to invest in the Fortescue-Homes Receptor? Or perhaps to *sell* on behalf of its owner/inventor? He supposed it would have quite a market as a kind of novelty fly paper, provided, of course, that it could be produced in sufficient quantities. He hoped the other nasty-minded nonsense could be discounted.

"You," the young man said, pointing his cigar at him in a very vulgar way, "you have got power. And so have I. You can see that for yourself," he jabbed the cigar towards the jar. "I've been wanting to get rid of her downstairs, Percy Phone or whatever silly name she calls herself, for some time. Tea leaves, I ask you! I can either give her the keys to the street, or – and this might be the more interesting course – if she turns awkward we could see just how much the jar *can* do. She won't be missed, I can guarantee that."

Mr Polkington was thinking over the implications of this when the young man became suddenly practical. "I could move that rubbish out of the front window, dress the place up a bit, and let you have the room downstairs, and we share the clients and the profits," he gave Mr Polkington a sharp, assessing look. "You could have the serious clients. The seekers. I'd deal with the daft women wanting to be told they're going to travel over water and meet a tall dark man on a Wednesday, and take care not to forget to put the cat out. I'm good at that."

Yes, Mr Polkington thought, *I'm sure you are.* The man was a charlatan, a fortune teller, preying on the sad and silly. But Mr Polkington knew that he was telling the truth when he said he had power. And whatever he had in that jar was real enough. Perhaps if he did go along with the young man's proposals he would find out what it was... and perhaps find out more about his own powers. Perhaps find a use for them beyond what had been shown to him in the teashop or the strange riverside tavern, perhaps something for himself ...

It was Mr Polkington's common sense that came to his rescue. Would he, he asked himself, arrange for the delivery of a consignment of *anything* to this young man without seeing the money paid over (in cash) first? He did not think so.

"I must think it over," he said.

But Mr Fortescue-Homes was shaking his head. "No. It's now or never, Mr P. I don't make an offer like that twice." He stood up suddenly. "Tell you what. I've got a client coming in five minutes. You sit here and think it over."

He huddled the jar back in its green silk cover and, carrying it with him, left the room before Mr Polkington could protest. And a horrified Mr Polkington heard the click as he locked the door behind him.

He sat quite still, listening to the sound of the young man's boots on the stairs. Then he swiftly examined the room. It took him a very little while to realise that there was no way out. A younger, more agile man – possibly a gymnast, not burdened by Mr Polkington's respectable clothing and footwear – *might* have contrived to climb out of one of the windows. If any of the windows could be persuaded to open. But, as he discovered, they were all nailed or wired shut, and while it was quite possible to break one of the large panes, the sound would surely draw the attention of Mr Fortescue-Homes much sooner than that of a potential rescuer.

Perhaps, of course, he should risk that. Simply smash a window and call for help. When help arrived he could explain that he had been locked in the room by an obvious madman… but that madman would be up the stairs long before a helpful passer-by could understand what was going on. Mr Polkington was quite sure that he could overpower the younger man. He might not be a gymnast, but he was a firm believer in the doctrine of *mens sana in corpore sano*, as Mr Fortescue-Homes clearly was not – his narrow shoulders and wretched complexion bore witness to that – but could he do so before Mr Fortescue-Homes took the chance to *see what the jar could do?* And he had little doubt that it could do a great deal.

He sat down. "Now, Polkington," he said to himself. "You got yourself into this and you must get yourself out. But what in heaven's name can the wretched lout *have* in that jar? Whatever it is he certainly *shouldn't* have it. But he *has* got it, and just at the moment he's got me."

He looked out of the window again. The street and the square beyond were depressingly empty, and there were no lights in any of the surrounding houses. If only a sturdy London policeman would walk along the pavement. Or anyone. Even a child sent on an errand, who could run for a policeman... Something scratched on the door. Mr Polkington jumped. "Who's there?" he exclaimed.

There was a curious hissing from the area of the keyhole. Mr Polkington hurried across the room, with uneasy memories of a certain story, read in a cheap magazine, of an attempt to despatch the hero by insinuating a snake into the locked room where he sat...but as he bent down to the keyhole he realised that it was not a reptilian hiss, but the word "Persephone," and came from human lips.

Ah. The lady from downstairs, the frightened lady whom the lout had called Percy Phone.

"Persephone!" Mr Polkington exclaimed rather too loudly.

There was an even more desperate hiss, presumably begging him not to draw Mr Fortescue-Homes' attention. He tried again, more quietly. "Persephone. Can you help me? Is there another key to this door?"

"No," her desolate reply came, hardly above a breath.

"Then," he whispered urgently, "you must run and fetch a policeman."

This suggestion produced nothing but a defeated whimper.

"Persephone," Mr Polkington insisted, "I would not ask you to do this but I fear my life may actually be in danger."

"The police can't help. He has the jar..."

"Nevertheless, I think we must..."

"It's no use," she moaned. "And they hate him so – he is *killing* them by what he makes them do."

"Killing – who is he killing?" Mr Polkington demanded.

"*Them*... he has *them* in the jar..."

"But who... *what* are they?"

Another thread-like gasp and then the word: "*Fairies.*"

Poor woman, thought Mr Polkington. He has quite literally frightened her out of her wits. It would most certainly do no good to send her for the police. They would never believe her.

"You must help them," she whimpered, "use your powers."

Mr Polkington shook his head. *Use your powers.* It was all very well to say that, but how? On the last two occasions when he had faced an unpleasant supernatural entity – once some kind of werewolf, once a demon conjured by a would-be black magician (who had now settled down to a life of gardening and good works, occasionally inviting Mr Polkington to supper in his delightful house in Chelsea) – he had been supported by the two ladies who had drawn him into their strange world, to say nothing of young Violet Throop and the beautiful Pearl – whose skills in unarmed combat would come in remarkably useful just now. He was not even sure he *could* use such powers for his own protection. And he could certainly expect no support from poor Persephone. But he must try at least. He had a sudden thought.

"Sometimes all the doors in a house can be locked with the same key," he whispered hastily. "Can you bring an assortment of keys and *try* them?"

"Yes, yes," she hissed, and he heard the creak of the stairs again as she crept away.

Perhaps the best thing he could do was wait by the window until Mr Fortescue-Homes' client left and try to attract his attention. This plan relied quite heavily on the client being a respectable person who would be willing to help, but surely...

There was a scratching sound from the keyhole, and he realised that Persephone had returned and was doing her poor best to unlock the door. He suspected that her fingers were trembling too much to make her task very easy. Once he heard a sharp rattle as she seemed to drop an entire handful of keys and spent an agonisingly long time scrabbling to pick them up. Then he heard her muttering to herself, "Oh I've tried that one already... or have I ... oh dear, perhaps I'd better drop each one as I try it... oh, no, that one's much too big," as she tried key after key.

"Persephone!" he called as softly as he could, "Persephone, this is not going to work. You mustn't let him find you trying to help me. Leave it now."

But the only reply was a gasp and a squeak. "I

think this one moved the lock a little... if I twist it..."

"Don't force it!" he gasped. "Ease it, gently..."

He heard her moan, "Oh dear..." but then he heard the grinding click of a turning key and the door swung open. But before Mr Polkington could make a dash for the stairs he heard a sneering and unpleasant voice from much too close at hand. Just behind Persephone's shoulder, in fact.

"Well, well, well, you've certainly got more sense out of old Percy Phone than I ever managed," he said, striding forward and forcing Persephone inside the study. He was carrying the jar, still veiled in green silk. "Made up your mind yet Polkington, or shall I see if the jar can manage two at once?"

Persephone gave a faint moan, and Mr Polkington made up his mind. He had played rugby in his younger days, and almost to his own surprise he found himself tackling Mr Fortescue-Homes low and hard. As he went down, Mr Polkington snatched the jar from his arms and fled down the stairs with it. He heard the sound of heavy boots behind him, suggesting that Mr F-H had recovered rather sooner than he had bargained for, but Mr Polkington discovered in himself a wholly unexpected turn of speed which carried him across the road and into the square. Surely, he thought, there was some kind of keeper or gardener there, or even one or two of the sort of people who hung about in such places for nefarious purposes, even they would do. What Mr Polkington needed was *witnesses* – witnesses, he felt instinctively would certainly cramp Mr F-H's style... but the square was empty. He pounded across it. This was London; somewhere, somehow, he would find people. Then a dreadful scream tore the still evening air, and he turned.

Mr Fortescue-Homes was standing at the gate of the square, his hand twisted in Persephone's hair. As Mr Polkington looked he jerked his hand and she screamed again.

"Stop," he shouted, "or I'll break 'er neck. I'll do it. I will."

"Let him," Persephone gasped. "Save them. I don't matter. I'm nothing but a silly old woman."

Mr Polkington turned back. "Let her go," he said.

"Give me the jar and I will. You can 'ave 'er,"

his mincing vowels were deserting him, along with his "h's", Mr Polkington noticed.

"Come now," he said. "What you are doing is not...not *manly*. Release the lady at once and we will discuss the jar."

Mr Fortescue-Homes eyed him, and probably deciding that there was not much more running in him, he released Persephone with another spiteful jerk at her hair, making her cry out again. She collapsed onto the path, sobbing. Then he advanced on Mr Polkington, fixing him with those dark, liquid eyes.

"Why don't you just hand over the jar, old chap?" he asked in a curiously warm, insinuating voice. "You know you want to. It's a bit heavy for you, isn't it... and dangerous... you can feel it's dangerous..."

Mr Polkington certainly could. As he clasped it against his chest it felt alive and very dangerous indeed, like a jam jar full of wasps. He would be more than happy to get rid of it.

Persephone raised her head. "Don't look into his eyes!" she called.

The young man snarled and aimed a kick at her.

"Ah. *Hypnotism!*" said Mr Polkington. He

looked firmly down at the glowing, silk swathed jar.

But that voice went on, weaving its evil magic. "Look here old boy," it said, "we can talk this over. Just put the jar down – carefully – there's a good chap. After all it is my property. My invention..."

Mr Polkington hesitated. He wanted to get rid of the thing. But he also wanted to *try* it. For a moment he was tempted to do what Mr Fortescue-Homes had suggested and *ask* for something. But what? A more satisfactory life? Excitement? Adventure? All the things he realised he had been longing for over the past month? Or – was anything possible? Could he have Ethel and Freddy back... Somehow he knew that would be the worst thing he could possibly ask for.

"No!" he said aloud. "Not this way!"

"Set them free!" Persephone called. "Break the jar."

"Don't – for all that's – don't..." shouted Mr Fortescue-Homes. "You don't know what they can do..."

"Well," Mr Polkington exclaimed, feeling suddenly wonderfully free and reckless, "let's find out, shall we?"

He lifted the jar with both hands and dashed it on the path at his feet.

There was what he could only describe, when he thought about it later, as a *soft* explosion. The glass certainly shattered, but it shattered into such tiny fragments that it drifted as a harmless, glittering dust through the grey air. And there was a great wave of light that split up instantly into dozens of tiny coloured lights that danced briefly round Mr Polkington's head before coalescing and sweeping towards Mr Fortescue-Homes. Mr Polkington thought he could hear dozens of small voices, all screeching hatred and vengeance.

"No," said Mr Polkington firmly. "You mustn't hurt him. You don't want to be as bad as he is, do you?"

The lights hesitated, flickered... seemed, perhaps, to confer...

"Just go free. That's what you want, isn't it? Take your freedom. If you take revenge you will *never* be free of him."

The lights swept up in a spiral and began to dance ecstatically through the trees. For some reason Mr Polkington remembered those lines from *The Tempest*:

Merrily, merrily shall I live now
Under the blossom that hangs on the bough...

He found himself smiling. And suddenly, blessedly, it began to rain, a light sweet shower that washed the dust from the leaves and sweetened the air – and surely those trees *were* blossoming. The square was full of the scent of lilac and honeysuckle.

Mr Fortescue-Homes struggled to his feet and shambled out of the square. Mr Polkington and Persephone watched him go

"We shall hear of him again," she said.

"I rather fear we shall," Mr Polkington agreed sombrely. He bent down and helped Persephone to her feet.

"It is only a light shower," he said. "I am sure you will not mind sitting under the trees on one of these benches and telling me what has been going on."

Persephone sank down obediently. "Mr Fortescue-Homes was a medium. A very good one. I went to one of his sittings, with a friend, and he called me out of the group. He...he...stared into my eyes, and I felt quite strange and faint, and afterwards my friend told me I had said all sorts of things. Oh, not *bad* things, but very strange ones about crystal cities, and...and...other planets, and...Atlantis... So he said I was a rare medium but *undeveloped*. And he said I should meet him for private sessions so that he could develop my powers."

Mr Polkington shook his head.

Persephone blushed and looked, for a moment, surprisingly young. "Nothing *wrong* happened between us. Ever. But he did persuade me that it was my *duty* to use my powers. For the good of humanity. He was very persuasive. I found out later that he used...he used to have a music hall act. As a hypnotist. And he knew I had a little money. I don't think I was the only lady he had taken money from."

"The scoundrel!" Mr Polkington exclaimed.

"Well. My family were quite opposed to our association. It was my brother who found out about the music hall act – he hired a private detective. So...so I ran away with him to London. I took this property, but most of my money is in trust and he couldn't get hold of it and he was very angry. I made some money by...by doing what I had done at the first sitting, allowing him to hypnotise me, I suppose, and talking nonsense to clients, but..." her lips trembled, "it wasn't enough. But he said he was in such need of money that he would try anything to get it. And he tried...he tried a conjuration he found in an old book for calling up fairies. It was horrid. He had to dabble about in hen's blood, and bury hazel sticks on Primrose Hill, and *call* the fairies by name. Some names worked and some didn't, but he caught quite a lot. The spell said he would be able to "command them to the utmost" – and he did. And then he didn't need me anymore, he said, but I couldn't go back to my family. I had quite cast off and anyway, I wanted to help *them*... I used to talk to them sometimes. I don't know if it *did* help..."

A cluster of lights swirled round her head and perched briefly on her hair.

"I think it did," Mr Polkington said. He did not argue the fairy question. Mr Fortescue-Homes had certainly imprisoned *something* in that jar, and whatever it had been was now rejoicing in the trees. It was as likely to be fairies as anything else, he supposed.

"I knew it was wrong," she pursued. "He had such *horrid* people coming to see him, and they wanted such *nasty* things. And he said as long as

I was there, I had to keep going into trances for them, when they wanted..."

"Shocking," said Mr Polkington. "But you will give all that sort of thing up now, will you not?"

"Yes," said Persephone with unexpected decision.

"What will you do?" he asked. "Shall you be afraid to go back to your..." he gestured across the road.

"My home," she said firmly. "No. He is beaten for the time being. He certainly will not come back tonight. Besides, he provided the place with excellent locks and bolts, and his keys were in his desk, not in his coat. I shall lock the doors, have a hot bath and a cup of tea, and tomorrow I shall clean the place from top to bottom. And on Monday I shall sell all the furniture in the study."

Mr Polkington was pleased to see her lift her hands to her hair and make some effort to re-arrange it. It suggested she was feeling more the thing... he noticed that the hair she was patting into place was surprisingly glossy, and surely much thicker than he had first thought. He wondered if those lights which had hovered over her had bestowed – capriciously, as he suspected they did everything – this favour of renewed youth and beauty.

"And then," she said, "I shall turn it into a teashop. Just as you thought it was."

"Quite right," Mr Polkington said. "I believe I can help you with that." He took out one of his own cards and wrote an address on the back. "If you need any kind of assistance, you will find me here. And if you go to the address I have written, I think you will find a lady who will help you even more."

Somehow he knew that she would find the teashop, and she would find it open and welcoming.

And the next time he went there, so would he.

Also by Tina Rath:

Collections

A Chimaera in My Wardrobe (Chivers Press, 2013)

As Editor

Conventional Vampires (Dracula Society, 2003)

*Now available and forthcoming from
Black Shuck Shadows:*

Shadows 1 – The Spirits of Christmas
by Paul Kane

Shadows 2 – Tales of New Mexico
by Joseph D'Lacey

Shadows 3 – Unquiet Waters
by Thana Niveau

Shadows 4 – The Life Cycle
by Paul Kane

Shadows 5 – The Death of Boys
by Gary Fry

Shadows 6 – Broken on the Inside
by Phil Sloman

Shadows 7 – The Martledge Variations
by Simon Kurt Unsworth

Shadows 8 – Singing Back the Dark
by Simon Bestwick

blackshuckbooks.co.uk/shadows